A book is a treasure we keep in our memory chest...
This treasure belongs to:

_____

To My Beloved, Who Was The Light of Day

Published by Faux Paw Media Group, A Division of Faux Paw Productions, Inc.™

Composed in the United States of America
Printed in Seoul, Korea

First Impression 2006
ISBN 0-9777340-0-5
SAN: 850-637X

Library of Congress Cataloging-in-Publication Data

Carman, Debby
I'm Gronk and I'm Green / written and illustrated by Debby Carman

Summary: 1. Dogs-Fiction   2. Stories in Rhyme. 3. Title.
I. Carman, Debby, ill.   II. Carman, Debby III. I'm Gronk and I'm Green

I'm Gronk and I'm Green

A parable written and illustrated by Debby Carman©

By the fact that I'm green,
Green as you've ever seen!

For a dog to be green, I mean.

do sniffers and snoopers

and PeePees and Poopers

do wiggles and waggers
and lickers and lappers."

"But don't roll in the grass please
you'll turn green and you'll sneeze."
My mother had told me,
My father would scold me.
I know I'm a dog and do the silliest things.

On that very day
In the dog park at play.
My mother had told me,
My father would scold me.
"If you must go to the park
for a run and a bark,

do woofers and whiffers,
and whiskers and kissers,
go romp and rollover
and sniffies in clover,
BUT don't roll in
the grass Please.
You'll turn green and
you'll sneeze!"

My mother had told me,
My father would scold me.
I know I'm a dog and
do the silliest things.

The sun was bright yellow,
the grass like a pillow,

While showing off for a Poodle
I went upsy doodle,

And lay in the grass,
Bright green for the spring.

I jiggled and flipped,
Jumped high, then I slipped

On the grass I went skidding,
Bright green for the spring.

Then I wiggled and rolled
Down the top of the knoll,

At the end of the romp
I swallowed a clump
of the bright greenest of grass,
Bright green for the spring.

And my mother who pleases
agreed there's a reason,

"The object in life,
grow up and be good,
be steady and ready
and do what you should."

Does everyone know what I mean?
My name is GRONK and I'm green.